This book belongs to

· · · · · · · · · · · · · · · · · · · · · · · · · · · · · · · · · · · · · · · · · · · ·

D0301177

First published in 2013 by Miles Kelly Publishing Ltd
Harding's Barn, Bardfield End Green, Thaxted, Essex, CM6 3PX, UK

Copyright © Miles Kelly Publishing Ltd 2013

2 4 6 8 10 9 7 5 3 1

**Publishing Director** Belinda Gallagher
**Creative Director** Jo Cowan
**Editorial Director** Rosie McGuire
**Senior Designer** Joe Jones
**Production Manager** Elizabeth Collins
**Reprographics** Stephan Davis, Jennifer Hunt, Thom Allaway

All rights reserved. No part of this publication may be reproduced, stored in a
retrieval system, or transmitted by any means, electronic, mechanical, photocopying,
recording or otherwise, without the prior permission of the copyright holder.

ISBN 978-1-78209-292-6

Printed in China

British Library Cataloguing-in-Publication Data
A catalogue record for this book is available from the British Library

## ACKNOWLEDGEMENTS

The publishers would like to thank the following artists
who have contributed to this book:

Cover (main): Mélanie Florian at The Bright Agency
Decorative banners (cover and throughout): asmjp from Shutterstock.com
Insides: Priscilla Lamont

Made with paper from a sustainable forest

www.mileskelly.net   info@mileskelly.net

**www.factsforprojects.com**

# The Frog Prince

Miles
Kelly

Once upon a time, there lived a very spoilt princess, who always got her own way.

One day she decided to

# The Frog Prince

play with her golden ball in the palace gardens. But she threw the ball too high, and it fell with a splash down a deep well.

The princess stamped her foot and yelled, but this did not help. So she kicked the side of the well, and a large frog jumped up out of it.

"Ugh," said the princess. "A slimy frog! Go away at once."

But the frog didn't move. Instead, it said, "Why are you making such a fuss?"

For a moment the princess

## The Frog Prince

was speechless with surprise, but then she said grandly, "If you must know, my precious golden ball has fallen down this well. I want it back."

With a great leap, the frog disappeared down the well. In the wink of an eye, it was back with the golden ball.

The princess went to snatch it up, but the frog put a wet foot rather firmly on it and said, "Have you never learnt the words 'please' and 'thank you'? Hasn't anyone taught you any

# The Frog Prince

manners? I have a special request to make of you."

No one ever dared talk to the princess like that. She glared at the frog, but then said crossly, "May I have my ball back, please, and what is your special request?"

# The Frog Prince

The frog said, "I want to come and live with you in the palace and eat off your plate and sleep on your pillow, please."

The princess was horrified, but she was sure a promise to a frog wouldn't count so

she agreed to the request.
Then she grabbed her ball
and ran back to the palace.
   That night the royal family
were having supper when a
strange voice called,
"Princess, where are you?"
and in hopped the frog.

# The Frog Prince

"Oh bother!" said the princess. The king frowned.

"Do you know this frog, young lady?" he asked.

The princess told her father what had happened. When he heard the story, he insisted the princess keep her promise.

The frog ate very little, the princess even less. When it was time for bed the king

# The Frog Prince

looked very sternly at the princess, who was trying to sneak off on her own. She sighed crossly, picked the frog up by one leg, and when she reached her four-poster bed, she plonked it down in the farthest corner. She did not sleep a wink all night.

The next evening the frog was back. Supper was a quiet affair. The king read the newspaper, and the princess tried not to speak to, or even look at, the frog. Bedtime came, and once again the princess had a restless night. By the third evening the princess was very hungry. She forgot to be rude to the frog and ate everything that was

placed in front of her. At bedtime she was completely exhausted, and fell asleep the very instant that her head touched the pillow.

The next morning the princess awoke feeling much better, until she remembered the frog. But it was nowhere to be seen. At the foot of the bed, however, stood a handsome young man in a green velvet suit. He said, "Hello, princess. Do you know that you snore?"

The princess's mouth fell

open ready to yell but the
young man continued. "I
don't suppose you recognize

# The Frog Prince

me, but I was the frog who rescued your ball. I am a prince, and I was bewitched by a fairy because I was rude and spoilt. The spell could only be broken by someone equally rude and spoilt having to be nice to me."

The king was extremely impressed with the young man's good manners, and the queen liked the look of his green velvet suit. Everyone liked the fact that the princess had become a much nicer person because of him.

# The Frog Prince

The prince came to live in the palace and after a few years he and the princess fell in love and got married. They had lots of children who were not at all spoilt and everyone lived happily ever after.

The End